The Global Warming Express

Story by Marina Weber
Pictures by Joanna Whysner

The Global Warming Express

Terra Nova Books
Santa Fe, New Mexico

The Global Warming Express (TheGlobalWarmingExpress.org) is a By Kids/ For Kids Think Tank Program for children ages 8–12 run by The Global Warming Express, a 501(c)3 organization.

The program is designed to be mentored by grownups but powered by kids, who decide what Big Goals and Small Goals they want to accomplish. Science—especially climate science—sustainable solutions, public speaking, writing, visual arts, and performance (theater, singing, and dance) are woven together to give the kids a platform of information and tools with which to make their voices heard.

If you would like to start a GWE summer or after-school program or order more copies of *The Global Warming Express* books for your school, home school, or summer program, or would like to contact our Kids Board of Directors, send an email to us at Genie@TheGlobalWarmingExpress.org.

Library of Congress Control Number 2017934496

Distributed by SCB Distributors, (800) 729-6423

Terra Nova Books

Published by Terra Nova Books, Santa Fe, New Mexico.
www.TerraNovaBooks.com

ISBN 978-1-938288-93-7

*To our third-grade teacher, Barbara McCarthy, who
started us on this journey.*

Contents

Foreword

My father used to say that every generation has a rendezvous with the land. We hold the land in trust. That is our legacy from those who come before us. It is our obligation to those who will follow us. We are stewards of this planet, and all its habitats and natural treasures.

Five years ago, Marina Weber contacted me. She told me she was working on a book about global warming, and asked for my help. Marina may have been very young, only nine years old, but she was determined. She was true to her word. She did write her book, and what a memorable book it has turned out to be.

Marina and her talented friend, Joanna Whysner, who has provided wonderful illustrations, have created a modern-day fable. In doing so, they are sounding the alarm about the very real challenge of climate change.

In their story, two young girls make their way to Washington, D.C., on a magical train. Their mission:

to tell the world that we must change. Their lesson: We can change if we all work together.

On each step of their journey, they meet some of the animals that have been hurt, orphaned, or both by climate change. They see the damage to our air, our water, and our land. From fire and drought in New Mexico to a hurricane in New York City, the message is clear. The planet is warming. The Earth is in peril. We all have to do something about it.

As Marina explains, we cannot continue to smother the planet in greenhouse gases. Our world is overheating. Without all of us doing our part, "the Earth can't kick its blankets off."

Marina and Joanna and their animal friends—including an exiled penguin named The Fluff, a scholarly parrot named Inoah, a black bear cub named Tomás, and a guardian angel canary named Croissant—keep going. Their journey across our nation is on a train fueled by hope. And their plea to all of us is: We have to keep going too. We can't give up either.

The Global Warming Express is a wake-up call on the great challenge of climate change—and one that I hope we will all hear.

Thank you, Marina, for a remarkable adventure story, and for reminding us, as my father did in his time, that we have to take care of our planet. We have to protect it for your generation, and for generations to come.

—Tom Udall, U.S. Senator for New Mexico

Acknowledgments

We would like to say thank you to many people who helped to make this book a reality.

Our parents, who supported the idea to write and illustrate a book; Amy Bianco, for so much help with the science; Maggie Blanchard, for the design; Senator Tom Udall, for writing the foreword; and Congressman Ben Ray Lujan, for listening to us and believing in us.

We also want to thank everyone who is part of the Global Warming Express movement, the Board of Directors, the Advisory Board, the interns, the volunteers, the wonderful donors, Dr. Leslie Lakind, Mayor Javier Gonzales, former Mayor David Coss, Councilman Peter Ives, and all the GWE kids everywhere. Thanks for jumping onboard and helping to make a difference.

—Marina 🦋 Joanna

Characters

Author **Marina Weber** was born in Seattle and now lives in Santa Fe, New Mexico, where she attends Desert Academy. Marina has been a passionate activist since she was six.  Marina plays herself in the story. She believes in righting wrongs and in helping others to be heard, seen, and assisted. She is also fearless and single-minded when it comes to completing her quest. On the journey, Marina learns a big lesson about the limited power of grownups and her own emerging power; and she learns that not every journey—in fact almost none—moves in straight lines or has the outcome you expect. Marina comes to believe in the power of the journey itself, and in the power of the journey-takers.

Illustrator **Joanna Whysner** also attends Desert Academy. She moved to Santa Fe from Sleepy Hollow, New York, when she was eight. Joanna has been a serious artist since she was  very young, and has won many prizes for her art. In the story, Joanna creates her world on paper, in line and color and form. Her sense of mischief and humor help her turn every drawing into a commentary. Yet Joanna's sense of fun is challenged by the terrible, real-life pictures she witnesses on the train. The journey prompts her to look beneath the surface of her images, and to find the courage to portray what is scary as well as what is nice. She comes to realize that the truth must be told, but that it can be accepted and even embraced.

 The **Fluff** is an Emperor penguin from Antarctica. The Fluff is a practical, take-charge fellow who realizes that there is something wrong in his world and he needs help to fix it.

Croissant is a canary who flies for the Pastry Express. He keeps the girls' parents informed of their whereabouts with yellow notes. You can see him in illustrations throughout the book.

Creamy is a harp seal who was born in Greenland and raised in the San Diego Zoo. She has a positive mindset and is compassionate to others, but she is challenged by all the problems she encounters on this journey.

Inoah is an Amazon parrot that Joanna keeps as a pet. Thanks to Inoah, all of the animals and the girls learn whatever they need to know about the causes and effects of global warming.

Tomás Ascension Leyba Gonzales is a black bear whose family has lived on the same mountains in New Mexico for generations. He and his friend, **Sally**, a Jemez Mountain Salamander, are rescued by the girls and brought aboard the GWE train.

 **Flora** is a polar bear from western Hudson Bay who makes her way overland to Glacier National Park. Flora is a tough little bear, but she learns that in order to move ahead, she needs to be flexible and optimistic.

Edgar is a mountain goat who lives in Glacier National Park. The loss of the glaciers and his alpine meadow have left him with nowhere to go, so he decides to join the journey.

 **Lauren** is a boreal woodland caribou who lives in Alberta, Canada. She is desperate to escape the moonscape her home has become with tar sands extraction going on and find a safer place to live.

Lady Athabasca is a whooping crane who spends the summers in her ancestral breeding grounds in Wood Buffalo National Park, Alberta, Canada. She graciously offers to escort the girls and their friends to the Gulf Coast of Texas to learn about the Deepwater Horizon spill.

At the Gulf they meet **Zolo**, a talkative little wood duck who lost his family during the Deepwater Horizon spill.

Bobbi Sue Sunfish is a green sunfish from Acorn Fork Creek in Kentucky. Bobbi Sue doesn't give a hoot about global warming, but when she realizes that efforts to slow it would also clean up the water, she decides to get on board.

Zingo is a brown rat who lives in the sewers of New York City. He is an old hippie in danger of becoming completely jaded until he meets Marina and Joanna. With the militant gleam back in his eye, he teaches the girls about the power of political activism.

KEY
fluff
Train
Wood Buffalo Park
Tar Sands
Glacier Park
California
Santa Fe
San Diego
New Mexico
Antarctica

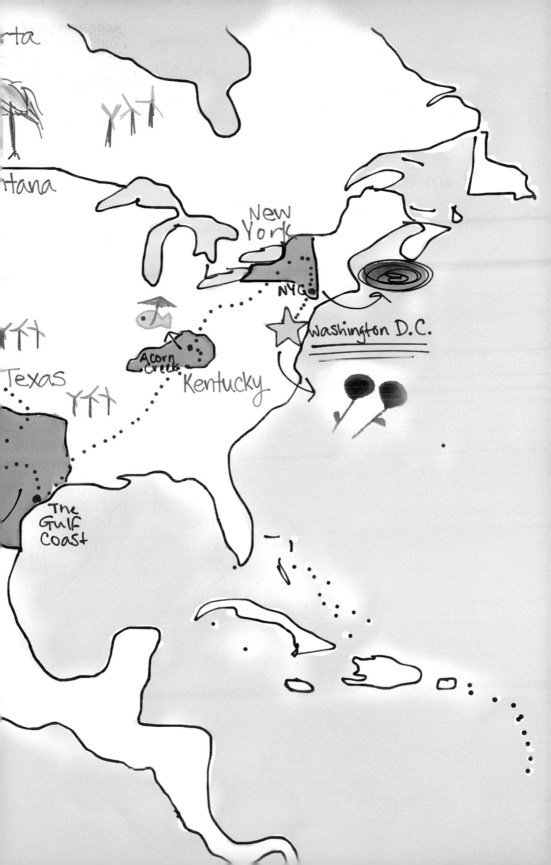

Introduction

Hello, my name is Marina, and I am here to tell you about global warming. I am in middle school at Desert Academy in Santa Fe, New Mexico. I have been interested in climate change since third grade, when I learned that global warming is ruining the habitats of animals in the rainforest. Global warming is a *very* important thing to me, because I want my children, grandchildren, and great-grandchildren to have happy lives without having to worry about the environment.

Our Earth is heating up mostly because of the gases we pump into the atmosphere when we burn fossil fuels to drive our cars, heat our houses, power our appliances, and manufacture things. We need to think about what we are doing to the Earth because it is changing fast! Now we have limited time to slow down global warming. Read on, and you will see what I mean.

I wrote to President Obama about climate change, and he always wrote back. At least, I *thought* he was writing me back, until one day I realized that all the replies I had received from him were pretty much the same.

Here is what one of them said:

THE WHITE HOUSE

WASHINGTON

April 8, 2010

Dear Student:

Thank you for your kind note. Your thoughtful words join a chorus of millions of Americans who are eager to lead our Nation towards a brighter tomorrow.

Each day, I am inspired by the encouraging messages of hope and determination I have received from students across the country. America needs young people like you who are studying hard in school, serving your community, and dreaming big dreams. Our country faces great challenges, but we will overcome them if we work together.

America's future will be determined by our willingness to support each other and move forward as one people and one Nation. With your help, we will build on what we have already achieved and lay a new foundation for real and lasting progress.

Sincerely,

3

Last year I learned that this is what is called a form letter. Probably a co-worker of the president's read my letters and wrote me back. Even though I hand-wrote my letters to the president, he obviously didn't read them. So I decided that I would write a book about global warming and bring it to the president!

This is my good friend Joanna. She is an amazing artist, so I asked her, "Joanna, I was wondering—and you can say no—if you would make some pictures to illustrate my book.

"I need to show how animals' habitats are being destroyed, so grownups will understand that we must do something about global warming. Dr. James Hansen, a famous climate scientist, told me that the animals are working hard to adapt to climate change, but I think they need our help. Will you help me?"

Joanna loved the idea of the book, and

she said, "Let's call it *The Global Warming Express* and invite other people to get on board!"

So now I am going to tell you about *The Global Warming Express* and our journey to see the president in Washington, D.C.

The story begins in Antarctica . . . .

The Fluff

On a warm, sunny spring afternoon at the Penguin Burial Ground on the shore of Queen Maud Land, Antarctica, a young emperor penguin named The Fluff wept for his mother. She had died after swallowing a piece of plastic floating in the ocean.

After the funeral, his colony offered their sympathies and departed, leaving The Fluff alone, sitting on a rock and gazing out to sea. He remembered sitting on this same rock when he was much younger, on a cold, sunny spring day when they had buried his grandfather. Now the rock was underwater, and the sun felt hot on his back.

"Why," he wondered, "is the water so high and the sun so warm?"

He took off his hat and scratched his head with his flipper.

"If this keeps up," he thought, "soon there will be no Burial Ground left."

The Fluff was very smart and had always been a great help to his colony. When another penguin had a problem, The Fluff always had a solution, but he could not understand what was happening to his land. Now, for the first time in his life, he felt a little afraid.

"As much as I hate to leave," he thought, "for the good of the colony, I have to find the answer to this!"

His father had been a penguin sea captain who was shipwrecked out at sea when The Fluff was really little. All that The Fluff had left to remember him by was his small lifeboat. The Fluff looked out to sea, feeling alone in the world. "I need to find my friend Creamy," he thought. "But how can I get to her?"

Bing! A light bulb went on in his head. "My dad's orange lifeboat!" he thought. "I can use that!"

The Fluff pushed off into the Weddell Sea as the sun was setting.

He rowed all day and floated on the current at night, dreaming of his meeting with Creamy. Upon waking one morning, he sighted land. He would later learn that he was in the Gulf of California.

Then The Fluff, who had lived all his life in cold water and ice, suddenly felt a warm southern breeze and smelled the delicious smell of shrimp. As he neared the shore, he knew he was a long way from home but a lot closer to his dear Creamy. Hungry, worried, and suddenly feeling *very* warm, The Fluff tied up his boat and went looking for air conditioning and a cold shower.

As he lay in his hotel bed that night, he wondered how he would find his friend. As far as he knew, she was still in the zoo in San Diego.

The Fluff fell into a deep sleep, filled with troublesome dreams. Images of his mother and father came and went as he tossed and turned. In every picture of his home, the ocean crept higher and higher. In the middle of the night, The Fluff awoke with a start. He sat up and realized that he needed more than

11

his old friend. He needed assistance from many others for himself and his world.

He needed help from those he had never trusted, or even met before.

Creamy

The next morning Creamy awoke in her plastic cave to the sound of crashing and banging. A ruckus had come up just outside her enclosure. Zookeepers rushed to and fro, yelling about a penguin that seemed to have escaped.

Creamy listened as the commotion got closer. A young penguin about the size of Creamy herself was waddling toward the seal enclosure where Creamy lived. As he opened the door with his beak and hurried in, he came up to Creamy and asked, "Where can I hide?" She hurried with the new penguin to some artificial rocks nearby. "I am Creamy," she told him.

The Fluff stared at her in amazement. "I found you at last!" he said. "Remember me? I visited you at the zoo when I was six years old while I was traveling with my father, the sea captain. I told you I would come back to free you someday."

"I remember you!" Creamy cried loudly. "You had feathers sticking out all over you!"

"Yeah, that's why my dad named me The

Fluff." Then he said, "Can you help me? I need help. My land needs help. You need help!"

Creamy was a harp seal. Like all harp seals, Creamy had been left on the ice where she was born off eastern Greenland when she was only twelve days old. She wasn't ready to swim yet when, because of global warming, the ice she was on melted too early. She would have drowned if two kind-hearted wildlife biologists hadn't found her in the water and rescued her. They sent her to the zoo in San Diego, California, and now she would never see her parents again.

Ever since then, Creamy had been wondering what was happening to the planet. She had always been very kind, and always tried to help those in need. Creamy came up with the idea of asking other animals in the zoo if they knew anything about what was happening to the planet. This way, she had found out lots about the environment.

Now The Fluff had found her, and they had a lot to talk about. They talked well into the night. They realized that they were both on their own now. They needed each other. And they needed to find a way to help the world stop changing so quickly.

They decided that they needed some kind of human transport out of the zoo.

"I've heard that there's an old zoo train that hasn't been used for over thirty years, but it might work," Creamy said. "We've always been told there's something special about it, but no one remembers what it is."

"Great," said The Fluff. "Let's go!"

The Magic Train

That night was the summer solstice, the longest day of the year. As darkness fell and the animals in the zoo quieted down, the two friends sneaked out of the seal enclosure. As they neared the machine shed where the abandoned train had sat unused for many years, they heard strange sounds, like grinding metal. Creamy looked at The Fluff, her eyes shining with excitement.

"Something wonderful is going to happen," she whispered. "I can feel it!"

Peering through the grimy window panes of the shed, they saw the train shake and shiver. They watched decades of dust and rust fall off its body until the old steam engine seemed to sparkle. Then the shed itself began to shake and rattle. The Fluff and Creamy were shaking and rattling too as they watched the train double in size before their eyes! Beautiful rainbow bubbles and fluttering butterflies filled the shed, and with a *crash!* the big doors flew open and the train moved into the clear moonlit night, stopping in front of the two friends.

The door of the first car opened, and before he knew what was happening, The Fluff felt Creamy push him onto the train. Creamy was right behind, clapping her flippers.

"Here we go!" she laughed.

With their noses pressed to the big window, they watched as the train lurched forward in the moonlight past the animal cages, through the sleeping city, and out to the ocean. Just as they thought they were going to ride right into the sea, the train turned sharply to the right and headed north up the coast.

"Wow!" The Fluff said to himself. "I wonder where we're going."

Exhausted from all the excitement, they both flopped into comfy seats and gazed out the window at the scenery speeding by.

After a while, The Fluff had a thought. "What does this train run on?" he asked. "I don't see any smoke."

"Look!" Creamy answered, pointing out the window.

Bubbles and butterflies had filled the air around the train. The sight of the beautiful bubbles and butterflies in the bright moonlight made them both feel very happy and hopeful. And as they did, the train seemed to shift into a faster gear.

"Why did we just speed up?" The Fluff asked. Then he had an inspired thought. "Oh, wait a moment!

Maybe when we think happy, positive thoughts, the train speeds up!"

"So then, if we're sad or negative, the train will slow down?" Creamy wondered.

"Let's try it," said The Fluff. "Think of a very sad thought. Think of—"

"—our parents," Creamy said.

They looked at each other with tears in their eyes. Then another jolt made them look out the window again. The train was moving very slowly. They stared at each other, eyes wide with understanding.

"I guess," whispered Creamy, "we better think positively."

"I think you're right, Creamy," said The Fluff.

"We can do this!" he shouted.

"Yes, we can!" shouted Creamy.

Then they both exclaimed, "Come on, you beautiful train, let's go!"

And once again, the train was surrounded by millions of bubbles and butterflies. It lurched ahead into the night, and almost seemed to fly!

New Mexico

The next morning, Creamy awoke just in time to see a sign that said, "Welcome to New Mexico."

"I wonder why the train took us here?" Creamy said.

"We'll have to wait to find out," The Fluff replied.

It was past midnight when they pulled up to an old, wooden gate in an adobe wall.

"Let's not get out yet," The Fluff said. "I have a feeling they will come to us, whoever they are."

Inside the house, Marina woke her friend Joanna. "I think there's something outside," she whispered.

"Uuuhhh. . .lee me lone," yawned Joanna.

"Joanna!" Marina shoved her off the bed.

"Okay, okay!" Joanna said as she got to her feet. "Should I wake up my parents?"

"Well . . . . ," Marina said, staring out the window. "I don't think so, but I think we had better get dressed." She put her finger to her lips.

"Squawk!"

"Oh, no," Joanna said. "We woke up Inoah. She never keeps quiet."

"Maybe we should bring her," Marina suggested.

Joanna quietly took the blanket off the top of the parrot's cage.

"No leaving without me! No leaving without me!" the parrot shrieked.

"Shhhh!" Joanna said as she unlatched the hook on Inoah's cage. The bird walked carefully up her arm and sat on her shoulder.

The girls silently opened the front door, only to find a penguin standing beside a train that sparkled in the night.

"Who are you?" the penguin and the girls asked at the same time. But before anyone could answer, the train began to move.

"Come on!" yelled The Fluff as he jumped in the open door. "We need you! The train found you because you can help!"

"What?" called Joanna.

The train was leaving. "Run!" Marina yelled. "Let's go!"

Before they knew it, they were being pulled on board. "I'm being pulled by . . . flippers!" Joanna said. And then they were inside the moving train.

Creamy and The Fluff told the girls how they had escaped from the zoo because they wanted to help other animals, but that they didn't know where the train was going.

"Going east! Going east!" Inoah interrupted.

"Hang on . . . . Maybe you were meant to pick us up!" Marina exclaimed. "Joanna and I want to meet the president of United States to tell him that global warming is hurting the animals, and it needs to be fixed right now."

"What does the president do?" The Fluff asked.

"He controls the United States," Marina answered.

"Well, then let's go together," Creamy said. "We want to make a change too!"

Fire

Inside the train, wisps of smoke floated through the air.

"What's that smell?" The Fluff asked.

"Oh," Marina said, "it's smoke from a forest fire. We've always had fires in the summer, but in recent years, there have been more. Joanna, it smells like your dad is cooking breakfast!"

Joanna smiled. "It's because global warming is causing terrible droughts in this area," she said, serious again. "New Mexico has been in a drought for years."

The train chugged into the Santa Fe National Forest.

"Oh, my!" Creamy said. "Is this what a *fire* is?"

Outside the window, the morning sun was gone, and the sky was gray. Flames rose above them, licking the tree-covered mountain. The girls and their new friends watched in horror.

"I think," The Fluff said quietly, "that since the train is magical, we can't get hurt. At least I hope so!"

Just then, they saw a black bear cub huddling under a tree. The crown of the tree was on fire.

The train stopped so suddenly that a door flew open. The group ran over to the little cub, who seemed to be sleeping.

"Let's pick him up, get him into the train, and then get out of here," The Fluff said.

The two girls carefully picked up the bear. They could barely see the train even though it was only a few feet away. Creamy could not stop coughing. As soon as they scrambled onto the train, it took off. The doors closed as smoke poured into the car, along with some of the train's bubbles.

As Joanna gently placed the little bear onto a seat, she noticed something in his paws.

"He's holding something," she said.

"But, his paws—they're burned!" Marina exclaimed.

The girls looked at each other in despair. Silently, The Fluff pointed to the bubbles. They were floating to the sleeping bear—and landing on his paws with a sparkle.

"That's incredible," Marina said. "His paws are healing!"

The train was already far away from the forest fire when the bear woke up.

"Who are you?" he said. "And what am I doing here?"

"You were . . . We are. . . ," Creamy began, but stopped when a little salamander jumped onto the floor. It was so small no one had even noticed it in the bear's injured paw.

"This is Sally. She's a Jemez Mountains Salamander," the bear cub said. "And my name, he added proudly, is Tomás Ascension Leyba Gonzales—but you can just call me Tomás"

"I'm special!" the little salamander squeaked as The Fluff awkwardly picked her up. "I am en-dane-gered!"

"Yes, *mi hita*, you are special," Tomás said fondly to the salamander.

"*Mi hita*," Inoah squawked. "Translation: sweet girl!"

Tomás smiled and explained that he had lost his parents in a huge fire the previous summer. The same area had been burned several years before, and the trees had not had time to recover.

"Now *los arboles* will probably never grow back," Tomás said sadly. "Sally and I are going to have to find somewhere else to live."

"*Arboles*!" Inoah screeched. "That means trees!"

"Oh, how awful!" Creamy exclaimed.

"Why don't you come with us," Marina said. "We are going to Washington, D.C., to tell the president he needs to do something about global warming. At least, I think that's where we're heading. This train seems to have a mind of its own!"

"A president?" Tomás asked. "What's that? And, um, while you explain, can you find me some food? I'm starving!"

The Greenhouse Effect

O ver lunch, Creamy asked Marina to explain this thing called global warming she had heard so much about.

"The Earth's climate has changed in the past twenty years or so," Marina said.

"But why so fast?" Creamy asked.

"Partly because of what humans have done," Marina said, "like making factories and cars. For the past century or so, humans have been using machines for just about everything. They've been burning stuff called fossil fuels—mainly coal, oil, and natural gas."

"*Burning? On purpose?*" Creamy asked.

"Yes," Joanna said. "We burn fossil fuels to make electricity for factories, and to heat and cool houses and buildings. We also use them as fuel for tractors, trucks, trains, airplanes, and cars. Now, our whole way of life runs on fossil fuels."

"Is that why the air and water sometimes get so dirty?" Tomás asked.

"Yeah," Marina said, "but that's not all. This burning—of the fossil fuels—is changing the whole atmosphere."

"Excuse me?" Creamy asked.

"The atmosphere is the air—what's all around us," Joanna explained. "It makes life on Earth possible by holding in heat from the sun. Without it, our planet would be a bare, cold rock or a burnt cinder, like the other planets."

"Planets?" The Fluff asked.

"Well, yes, I'll tell you more about that later," Joanna said.

The animals fell silent and looked puzzled.

Inoah broke the silence: "There are gases in the atmosphere—carbon dioxide, water vapor, methane, nitrous oxide, and others—that trap sunlight so it can't radiate back into space. This is like the sunlight in a glass greenhouse that makes plants warm even in the winter, so it's called the greenhouse effect."

"A greenhouse?" Creamy asked. "Where is it?"

Suddenly, a ripping sound came from the far wall, and a screen like the kind you show movies on rolled down with a *snap*! It began showing them moving pictures like a video, only they realized it was real. The screen seemed to be magically showing them what was happening outside the train, but in more detail.

"Wow!" said Marina and Joanna at the same time.

"That's what greenhouse gases must look like!" Marina said.

"To a chemist," Joanna added.

The screen glowed with color. Layers of red, gray, and mustard yellow flowed in and out of each other.

"Usually, we can't see carbon dioxide," Marina explained as she pointed at the screen.

"Plants absorb carbon dioxide to grow. That's how they make their food," Joanna said.

"So it's good?" Creamy looked from one girl to the other.

"Yes, it's good," Marina answered. "The problem is that we've been producing too much CO_2."

"CO_2: short for carbon dioxide," Inoah interrupted.

"The plants can't take it all in," Marina continued. "So now, the extra CO_2 and other greenhouse gases are stuck in the Earth's atmosphere and are trapping too much heat."

"Ick!" said Creamy and the Fluff together as they looked at the swirling gases on the screen.

"How do you get rid of it?" Tomás asked.

Inoah piped up again: "There are many methods of carbon sequestration—"

"Another time, Inoah," Joanna said firmly. "Let's just say it's much better to avoid making too much of it in the first place."

"My friend Flynn told me the greenhouse effect is like this," Marina said. "Imagine you're in bed and you have all your blankets on, and then you get too hot, so you kick them off. That feels better, right? Well, that's how the Earth is, but the Earth can't kick its blankets off, so it just gets hotter and hotter. That's global warming, and it's not good!"

Flora

Joanna was up early the next morning. Still in her pajamas, with Inoah on her shoulder, she found the refrigerator and poured herself some juice. Then she settled into a comfy chair in the observation car to watch the sun rise over some spectacular, white-capped mountains. A sign whizzed past. It said, "Welcome to Glacier National Park."

As the train sped into the snowy landscape, Joanna saw a large white snowball begin to roll down a hill, causing a minor rockslide. She watched as the giant snowball rolled onto the tracks and stopped. The train lurched to a sudden halt, and Joanna heard bumps and moans from the sleeping car.

Creamy shuddered at the thought.

Flora was staring at Inoah. "What is *that?*" she asked.

"This is Inoah. She's a parrot," Joanna said. "She knows everything about everything, even polar bears."

"You don't say!" Flora said sarcastically. "Anyway, my parents told me the ice has been melting earlier and earlier in recent years, cutting our feeding time even shorter. We're starving!"

"Here," Marina said. "We'll show you to the dining car. You can just ask for what you want, and it will appear."

"Oh, cool," said Flora as she headed to the door.

A few minutes later, with her mouth full of

berries, Flora mumbled, "I game bere from bestern Budson Bay."

"Excuse me?" Sally piped in.

Flora swallowed her mouthful. "I came here from western Hudson Bay. I've been swimming and wading for months, looking for ice because last spring, the ice broke up early. My parents were swimming, and I got trapped by myself on a small patch of sea ice that had broken away from the main sheet. It was so scary! I saw my parents get smaller and smaller as the current took me far away. It happened so fast. It was too far to swim back. I didn't know what to do!"

Flora explained a little more: "I live—well, I used to live—in an igloo. It was very nice. My dad ran a local business, and my mom ran a preschool for polar bear cubs. I had lots of friends. So anyway, I thought that if I could just keep floating, I'd eventually hit land, but I was worried that my little patch of ice might melt away first. I waited for two sunsets and two sunrises, then I decided to jump off and swim to find land. I came down a long river and then to this land. I've been walking and walking through these snowy mountains till I fell down and rolled all the way to you!"

"Wow. What a story!" Creamy said. Her eyes were filled with tears. "I'm so sorry you had to go through all of that!"

She stood up and hesitated a moment, and then she gave Flora a big hug.

Edgar

The train had been climbing steeply while Flora talked. At last, it ground to a halt on a huge, pebbly lump of ice. All around was deep, frozen snow. Creamy and The Fluff practically flew off the train, tumbling over each other in their hurry.

"Let's go out in the snow!" they cried.

Flora followed after them, heading for the ice. Marina, Joanna, and Inoah followed, all shivering. Suddenly Flora caught sight of something. On a rocky ledge above their heads towered a large, white animal with pointy horns, peering down at them.

"Hi. I'm Edgar." He easily leaped down to

join them. "I'm a mountain goat. And you are . . . ?" he looked at them questioningly.

The animals and girls took a step back. Quickly, The Fluff introduced them.

"It's good to see ice again," Flora smiled.

"This ice is snow that melts and refreezes every year and then gets packed down," Edgar said in a deep, rumbly voice. "The whole thing creeps down the mountain, with new snow added at the top and water melting out the bottom. Scientists come up here every summer and measure it because it's shrinking."

"Just like the ice floes in my bay," Flora said.

"Scientist predict that all the glaciers here in Glacier National Park will disappear in the next ten or twenty years," Inoah announced.

Edgar shook his head slowly. "Then the summer streams will dry up," he said.

The tears began to roll from Creamy's big, black eyes as she listened.

Edgar's voice was sad as he talked more: "The animals and plants here are used to living in certain places on the mountain. As the summers get warmer, we all keep moving farther up where it's a little cooler. This is called migrating, but there's nowhere else for us to migrate to. We already live at the top of the mountain, above the tree line. Now the trees are growing up here, so they make shade that keeps the grass

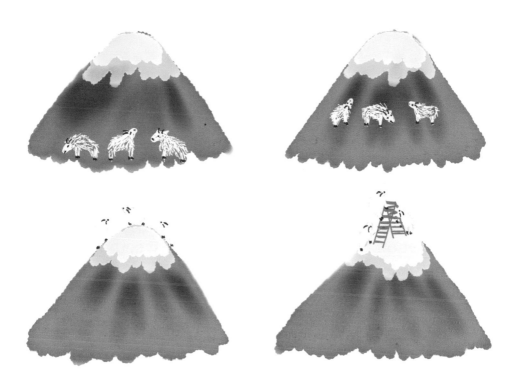

from getting the sunlight it needs, and it dies. Soon there'll be nothing for us to eat."

"So what are you going to do?" Tomás asked.

"You could come with us," Marina said.

"Ah . . . that's very kind of you," Edgar said, "but I've lived here all my life."

"I know how you feel," Tomás said. "I had to leave my mountain too. We have to adapt."

Edgar looked back at his meadow and sighed, and silence fell.

"We're all traveling together now because we need help," The Fluff explained. "We can't go home again until we get some help to save our lands."

"And ourselves," Flora added.

"I see what you mean," Edgar said. "I hate to leave, but . . . someone needs to know about our problems."

"We're going the see the president of the United States," Marina said. "He will help!"

"What's a president?" Edgar asked.

Joanna smiled. "We'll explain as we go. Come on! Let's get on the train. The sooner we leave, the sooner we'll get help!"

"Help! Help! Help!" squawked Inoah as everyone trudged to the open door of the train.

The Tipping Point

As the train started up again, The Fluff moved over to stand next to Marina.

"Where exactly is Washington, D.C.?" he asked thoughtfully as he watched the mountain landscape go by the window.

"It's on the far East Coast of this country," Marina told him. "It's a big city where all the grownups who are in charge of running the country work. That's where the president lives and works."

"Oohhh," The Fluff said. "Did he always live there? Or did he migrate?"

Marina laughed. "Well, I guess you could say he migrated! He was sent to live there by the people of America. It's called being elected. He

49

was chosen to lead the country, and so he moved with his family to live in Washington. He'll be there for a while and then move out."

"And then someone else will migrate there and be in charge?" The Fluff asked.

"Yep," Marina said. "We don't know who that will be. And we can't wait. We need to get *this* president to listen to us *now*."

"It feels to me like the train is heading north," Flora called out.

"I wonder where it's taking us?" Marina said. "I hope we turn east soon. We're running out of time!"

The train had come down out of the mountains and was crossing a wide, flat plain. Marina spotted an oil rig on the horizon.

"See that?" she pointed. "It's a machine for pumping oil out of the ground."

Inoah piped up: "In conventional oil fields, the oil is pooled under the ground, and machines drill down and pump it up. Natural gas can be drilled this way too."

"Humans have already burned up most of the fossil fuels that can be drilled or mined so easily," Marina added.

Inoah ruffled her feathers and continued loudly: "Now, energy companies are looking for other, more difficult ways to get at fossil fuels, like drilling deep in the ocean and in remote natural preserves."

"I know what preserves are—yum!" Joanna said.

With a deep sigh, Inoah corrected her: "Not that kind! We're talking about land that is preserved, kept safe, and treasured. Get it?"

"The oil companies are even drilling in that special land because for them, the treasure is the oil," Marina added.

"Like where I lived in the middle of arctic wilderness," Flora cried. "There are all these people there, with big machines, digging trenches and building pipelines!"

"Please!" Creamy cried. "This is so bad! Do we have to talk about it? The train is slowing down a lot."

"But you need to know!" Inaoh replied. "It's important to know the facts!"

Everyone looked at each other in sad silence.

"Then we have hydro-fracking for natural gas and squeezing oil from tar sands . . . ."

Suddenly the picture changed. Instead of forests and dark earth, there were miles of dead trees. In some places, they'd been removed, and the land was completely gray, the color of concrete. New "lakes" the girls and animals looked at were yellow-green as if they were sick instead of being a beautiful green-blue, or they were black with oil, or even a weird orange-green color. But the sky looked even worse. Thick plumes of smoke from countless smokestacks filled the air around miles of pipes. Then the screen snapped shut, and the train slowed down.

Outside the window, the passengers were looking at what they had last seen on the screen. Right in front of them seemed to be huge rivers and lakes, but they were filled with thick, gooey liquid that was black or orange. Suddenly, a big thundering sound shook the train. Giant machines and massive trucks appeared, moving across the empty land. The trucks and machines were so big they made the train look like a toy. They looked like skyscrapers on wheels, blotting out the sun. Just the wheel of one machine was more than thirty feet high. The noise became almost unbearable.

Then the train stopped dead in its tracks. Everyone looked around, confused and frozen in place. Creamy was crying. *"I don't like this place!"* she yelled (the only way to be heard). *"Do we have to stop here?"*

"It looks like the train wants us to stop here," The Fluff called out, "perhaps to meet more animals."

No one moved. The sky outside the window became darker, and an even louder rumble shook the train. Everyone put flippers, hooves, wings, and hands to their ears. They looked to where the sound was coming from, across an enormous hole in the ground, and saw a massive earthslide. It lasted for what seemed like an hour. Finally, there was silence.

"Um," Joanna said. "We have company."

On the other side of the train, a large head filled the window. It was one of the animals they had seen from the air. Her eyes were wide, and her nostrils were flaring.

The Fluff was the first to get out the door. "Come on!" he called to the others.

In a moment, the animals and girls had surrounded the frightened animal. The Fluff reached his flipper up to pat her shoulder.

"It's okay," he said. "We can help. My name is The Fluff, and these are my friends. This is called a train, and it's taking us on a journey to help other animals. This is Creamy and Flora. There are other animals on the train too. We also have two human children, Joanna and Marina. They're okay; they're on our side too."

"My name is Lauren, and I'm a caribou," the newcomer said. "And it's getting really dangerous here!"

"How can anyone live here?" wailed Creamy. "It's so dirty and awful."

"I feel so bad for you," Flora cried. "I thought what had happened to me was the worst, but now . . . ."

"They all lost their parents," Marina explained. "Their lands are also changing for the worse. Do you want to come with us to escape this horrible place?"

"Unless . . . you have family here that you don't want to leave?" Joanna asked.

"My family is in the far north by now. I left them to start my own life," Lauren said, "but this is no place to live."

Marina's face lit up. "We might have seen your family!" she exclaimed. "We saw more caribou walking north across some beautiful land."

"Yes, it may have been my herd," Lauren answered. "They move around a lot now that our habitat is in danger. This whole area used to be boreal forest, and what we in Canada call muskeg, which are peat bogs. Then the people from the energy companies came in and started ripping it up to get at the tar sands below."

"Tar sands are bitumen," Inoah piped up, "a highly viscous form of petroleum. Also known as asphalt, traditionally used as blacktop on roads. Hence the term 'tar' sands."

"Whatever it is," Lauren said wearily, "it's very heavy, gooey stuff. To get it to flow into a pipeline or onto a truck, the people blast it with river water that they've heated. Then they put the dirty water into some sort of ponds—"

"Tailing ponds!" Inoah interjected.

"—and they sometimes leak into the little streams in the bog, and eventually into the big river there. That's the Athabasca."

"I don't understand it. It seems like an awful waste of land," Edgar said.

"I did a science project on this," Marina said. "The energy companies claim they will restore it when they're finished."

"But there's no way they can replace the muskeg," Lauren said sadly. "It takes thousands of years to develop from slowly decaying plants like moss, which is what I eat. They're going to replace it with fake little hills and ponds."

"It sounds a lot like the room I lived in at the zoo," Creamy piped in.

"They shouldn't be doing this!" Marina said angrily. "This is not the zoo. This is a wilderness! We shouldn't even be burning the oil they're going to get from this, because it will produce too much CO_2. Not only that, but my research said that when they dig up the peat bogs, they release tons of CO_2 directly into the air."

"CO_2 again," Joanna echoed.

"The train has been stopped here a long time," Flora suddenly noticed.

"We need to keep positive to get it moving again," said The Fluff.

"How can we keep positive?" cried Creamy, "when we know that so much is wrong? This Tar Sands place is absolutely *horrible*!"

"Well," The Fluff noted quietly, "look at what we've done already. We've all traveled thousands of miles to get here, and now we have this train to help us!"

"And it's brought us together," Flora added. "Together, we can accomplish . . ."

"Anything!" said Sally. "Creamy, we *can* help all the animals in the world! Just like you want to!"

"Well, I know you helped me," Tomás said.

"And me," said Edgar.

"You came for me at just the right time," Lauren said.

The animals all smiled at each other. Joanna, who was holding Sally, looked over at Marina. "I just don't get where we fit in," she said. "You all have gone through so much hardship and we haven't. We're people, and people have caused this whole problem!"

"It's all our fault," Marina agreed. "People have been stupid. I mean, incredibly stupid. I don't really know *what* we're doing on this train anymore."

Usually, she was not the type to give up, and as Marina walked away with her head down, the animals got worried. Everything was quiet. A little yellow bird fluttered against the window, but no one noticed.

"I know what you're doing here!" Sally squeaked suddenly. She motioned for Joanna to lift her high so the others could hear. "You're listening to us. You're supporting us. You're helping us!"

"Yes," The Fluff said. "I knew when I left my home that I would have to find people and learn to trust them. From the ones I met in Antarctica, I could see that they were in charge—well, maybe not in charge, really, but they were more powerful than animals."

"And we knew that we needed help, and the train came along, and then it brought us to you two," Creamy said.

"And you're going to your Great Leader," Flora said. "You'll find us the help we need."

Even Inoah blurted out a reassuring squawk, "Yes!" Then she slapped her wings to her beak. She had surprised herself with her sudden emotional outburst.

Marina looked up at her friends. "I don't see how this is going to work, but if you believe there's hope, after everything you've been through, then I guess we should see where this journey leads us."

Everyone looked at her and at

each other, and one by one got back on the train. Once again, bubbles began to fill the air. The train started moving, slowly at first and then picking up speed.

Suddenly Flora jumped up. "Hey! Where's Creamy?"

Everyone looked out the windows. Creamy was running toward them.

"Seals can't run fast on their flippers!" Flora exclaimed. She pushed the door open, jumped off the moving train, and grabbed up Creamy in her arms. Then with her strong legs, she started bounding to the train.

"They'll never make it!" Sally squealed.

The Fluff had an idea. "Hey!" he cried out. "If we're sad, the train will slow down!"

Everyone began to cry—pretending at first and then really crying to think of losing their friends. The train screeched to a stop, dead still. Flora climbed on, still carrying Creamy.

Creamy was scared and relieved. Flora was winded. Everyone was very happy.

"Flora, thank you so much! You saved me! I would have been left behind. You're amazing!" Creamy said.

Flora hugged her.

Once again, now that they were all so happy, bubbles started coming out of the smokestack, and the train began to speed along. Flora and Creamy settled down next to each other.

"That is one odd friendship," Edgar observed. "But since I've been on this train, some pretty strange things have happened."

The rest of the animals headed off to get ready for bed. As night fell, they knew they were still moving through the countryside because there were no lights. Soon, they could hear water rushing outside, even louder than the clicking train wheels.

"We're following the Athabasca River," Lauren said sleepily. "It is a great river that my herd relies on for

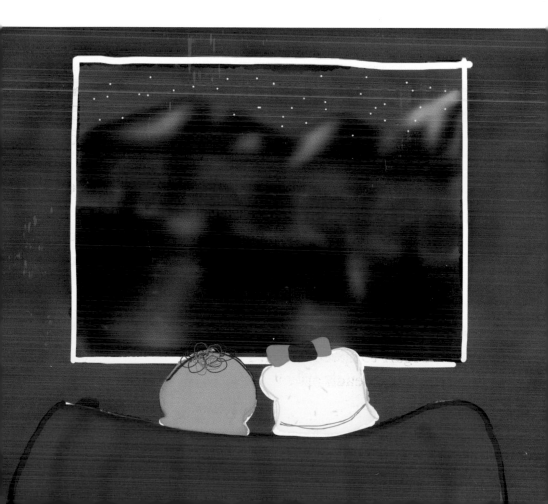

water. It flows north. I guess"—she yawned—"we are also headed north."

One by one, everyone settled down to sleep. It had been a long day. Only The Fluff continued to gaze thoughtfully out the window, his chin on his flipper, listening to the sound of the water rushing by.

Lady Athabasca

It was quiet when the girls and animals awoke at dawn. Lauren said, "I think we're nearing the mouth of the Athabasca River, the Peace-Athabasca Delta—"

"The largest freshwater inland delta in the world!" Inoah announced.

"This is Wood Buffalo National Park," Lauren went on, ignoring the parrot. "No machines are allowed here. It's a preserve for the wood buffalo and the whooping cranes—"

"Who almost went extinct," Inoah added.

"This is their only natural nesting habitat, but with help from the humans—lots of help—they've been able to adapt to other protected places," Lauren said. "Their winter home on the Texas Gulf Coast is also a sanctuary."

Suddenly the train came to a halt just in time to avoid running into a very large white bird sashaying across the tracks in a blue feather boa and purple

feather hat. She waved at them politely with one long wing.

"Eight feet!" Inoah squawked. "That's how long her wingspan is!"

"About ten times longer than yours is," Flora said drily.

Then Flora called out of the window: "You're a whooping crane, aren't you, ma'am?" The bird looked startled to be addressed by a polar bear.

The Fluff came to the train door and opened it. "Hi! We were just talking about you, or rather, your people, or, er, birds. Come in—I mean on."

The whooper graciously declined his offer. So The Fluff climbed down as the other animals watched and strolled around with the great bird.

As the whooper talked, The Fluff did his best to keep up with the crane's tremendous strides. Creamy giggled. Eventually, the two birds shook wings—or rather, wing and flipper—and The Fluff came back on board.

"Well? What did she say?" Creamy asked.

"I'll tell you soon," The Fluff answered, "but right now, we have to follow her. Her name is Lady Athabasca. I told her about our journey. She is joining her migration flock of nineteen other cranes as they head south. We need to follow them carefully, because they have something to show us."

"But their migration takes about two to three weeks!" Inoah exclaimed.

"I don't think we have three weeks to spare," Marina said. "Better tell her we can't go."

"What if we get them on the train instead, and we can be there in a couple of hours?" Flora asked.

"Um, Flora? I really don't see how we could fit twenty birds with eight-foot wingspans on this train," frowned Tomás.

"I know! I know! I know!" squeaked Sally. She was so excited she was jumping up and down a foot in the air.

"How does she do that?" Edgar asked.

"What is it, Sally?" Joanna asked, picking her up and holding her out so they all could hear her.

Sally was out of breath from all her jumping. "Put . . . (puff puff) . . . them (puff puff) on . . . (puff puff puff puff puff puff . . . .)"

"On *what?*" interrupted Flora. "Sally, what are you trying to say?"

"On the *top* of the train!" Sally managed to squeak, frowning her miniature eyebrows together at Flora.

"On top of the train. . . ," everyone repeated, looking at each other.

"Right," The Fluff said. "They can tell the train where to go and just ride there on top."

"And we all know that the train can go as fast as it wants to," Marina said.

"Especially when we're feeling happy and positive!" Creamy added.

"Great idea, Sally!" Tomás said as he gave her a salamander-sized version of a high five.

Marina went out to explain the idea to the big bird. Everyone watched as Lady Athabasca went off to talk with her flock. When she returned, the girls and animals all came out of the train. They peered upward as first Lady Athabasca, then nineteen more giant birds landed lightly on the roof of the train. Then they settled into sitting position as if they were all hatching eggs.

"Hey, if we're going to be moving fast, they're going to need seat belts!" Tomás said. On cue, the belts mag-

ically appeared over each crane's back and attached to the roof.

Lady Athabasca looked down her long nose—or rather, beak—at all the others. "This is a highly unusual circumstance, but . . . we are ready," she announced.

At this, the train jerked forward, and everyone else crowded aboard as it picked up speed. Lauren held out a hoof and pulled The Fluff in last.

"Wow," he called, "this must be what flying feels like!"

"We need a skylight to see them!" Tomás said. "I've never seen cranes fly without flying!"

"You've never even seen cranes, Tomás," Sally reminded him.

A skylight the size of the whole roof appeared. Above, the cranes were chatting with each other as if they did this every day.

"Well, I guess this will be the easiest migration these guys have ever had," said Edgar.

The Gulf Coast

As the animals were settling in for the journey, the train began to move very quickly. Flora noticed that the floor of the car had suddenly become transparent as well. She peered down at the earth moving along below, just as if she were looking through ice. "Look, everyone," she shouted. "We can see the ground!"

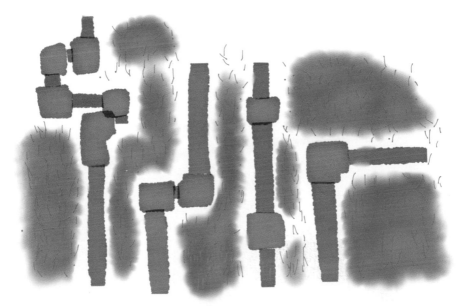

They all looked down and then out beyond the train at giant pipes running straight across the land.

"It looks like thousands of Tinkertoys," Joanna observed.

"Yeah, but they're real," Marina answered, "and way more dangerous than Tinkertoys. They bring oil down to ports on the Gulf Coast, and from there, it's sent all over the world to be burned! I studied all about it."

"Lady Athabasca was telling me about this," The Fluff said. "It's called the Keystone Pipeline System. The cranes fly over it twice every year when they migrate, so they know it well. She said that sometimes, the pipes break and leak oil onto the land and into the streams and lakes. It's especially dangerous for Lady

Athabasca and other water birds, because if they get covered with oil they can't swim or keep warm, and they die." He looked down sadly.

The train followed one of the great pipes to what looked like a huge factory, belching smoke.

"What's that?" Flora asked.

"It's a refinery," Marina explained. "It's where the crude oil is made into gasoline for cars, and other things."

"Does it involve . . . burning?" Creamy asked.

"Yes," Inoah squawked. "They have to heat the oil up to 400 degrees."

"Fahrenheit," Joanna added.

"What height?" Flora asked.

Just then, the screen rolled down to show them images of oil being burned all over the country, creating a cloud of CO_2 and methane that seemed to fill up the air all the way to outer space.

"See?" Marina said. "That's why we have no time left. We have to convince the president to stop all this. Now! There's no room for more of that."

"Yes, but we're heading south now, not east," Flora pointed out.

They had only been traveling for an hour, but they could see through the bottom of the train that they were now over sand. Out the window, as the train began to slow down, the view was of an approaching shoreline.

"This must be the Gulf Coast of Texas, where the birds migrate for the winter," Joanna said.

In a moment, the train came to rest on a beautiful beach. It was sunset.

The seat belts disappeared into the air, and the cranes gracefully rose up, stretched, and flew down to the water to drink and fish. The other animals followed.

"Oh, how gorgeous," Marina said. "Beaches are my favorite thing!"

Everyone looked out at the peaceful scene of a flock of whoopers wading through the water.

"Let's swim!" Flora said.

Everyone who could swim, did. Creamy, Flora, and The Fluff had such a great time that they didn't want to get out of the water. As darkness fell on the Gulf, they were the last to come back to shore.

"That was perfect!" The Fluff said. "Even if it was a little warm for my taste."

"Look," Joanna said. "The cranes want us to follow them."

In the near-dark, the cranes had all risen from the sea and were waving to them. Lady Athabasca landed and explained, "If we hurry, we can show you something else we wanted you to see."

She began leaping with her long legs and scooped up Sally in her wings. Everyone ran after her. Some of the animals were really fast. Marina and Joanna rode on Tomás and Flora, while Creamy and The Fluff hitched a ride on Lauren.

"You're ruffling my feathers!" shrieked Inoah from Joanna's shoulder, holding onto her straw hat.

A few minutes later, they had joined the whoopers on the edge of the darkening Gulf. The full moon glittered on the waves, except in places where the water was completely dark.

and then she said and I was like he said OMG! I mean lik cool hat and he was like WOW there's a spider on your head!

Lauren looked startled. "Hey, what's that in the water? I've seen that stuff before! I even drank some once, by accident. Don't tell me that this just like the Tar Sands!"

"Well, yes, it is, after a fashion. That's the problem," Lady Athabasca said. "This is what we wanted you to see. This is oil, dumped by a huge oil spill. Three million gallons of oil. It came from the explosion of an offshore oil rig called the Deepwater Horizon. It's killed many beings, including some humans."

"Oil again?" Lauren said unhappily. "I thought I was getting away from oil."

The moon went behind clouds, and the night was completely dark. The animals, who had been joyful— at least for a little while—now walked sadly back to the train. Only The Fluff remained behind. Seeing the way the ocean was affected here brought back memories of his endangered homeland.

"First, the plastic, then the melting ice, now oil," he said aloud. "If there was ever a time to make this all stop, it's now. I must tell Marina that we need to get to her president right away! We need to tell him this is all because of those things called fossil fuels! It's all their fault! He needs to help!"

"Well, I could use some help," a small voice replied. Looking down to where the sound came from, The Fluff saw a tiny, green and brown duck illuminated in the moonlight, bobbing in on the gentle waves at the shore.

The Fluff bent down to see the little creature, who looked up at him in relief.

"Zolo! My name is Zolo! You are the biggest, most gigantic duck I have ever, ever seen! Did you come to save me? My family is gone! I have no one left! There is still oil on my feathers or I would fly away, back to where my grandma lives! Can you help me? What's your name? Where did you come from? Do you have oil on you too? And why is your beak so long?" the little guy said in one breath. Then, finishing off his thought, he added, "I really like your hat."

Smiling, The Fluff didn't say anything. He gently picked up the tiny duck and sat down, holding him in his flipper. Soon, the little guy was asleep, but The Fluff stayed awake for a long time, gazing thoughtfully out to sea.

Next morning, one by one, Marina, Joanna, Tomás, and Sally made their way to the cove. (Creamy and Flora couldn't resist one more swim, and had been far out in the ocean for hours.) On their way to the cove, the girls and animals met The Fluff walking toward them, looking as though he were talking to himself. As he got closer, though, they realized he was talking with a very small being walking beside him.

"Don't let him start talking," The Fluff warned in a whisper as they all came together. "He never stops!"

Suddenly, a whistle blew from farther up the beach. The train, with a mind of its own, was starting to move off without them! Out of the water in a flash came the polar bear and seal. Everyone else ran to catch the train. Joanna was the last to jump aboard. She turned to see the whoopers, all standing in the shallow surf. Lady Athabasca raised a wing, and suddenly, all twenty whooping cranes waved their wings in a sort of salute. "Goodbye!" Lady Athabasca called. "Now that you know about this, you can help find the solution for all the water birds. Poor dears! Good luck!"

"Good luck to you!" Joanna called out. With a tear in her eye, she clambered onto the moving train.

Onboard, the others watched the cranes and the beach disappear into the distance.

"It sure was nice to be in the ocean again," Creamy said wistfully. She looked over at Flora, who looked over at The Fluff. But The Fluff was busy. He was helping the little duck to remove what looked to be a very dirty, very old bandage.

"What happened to you?" Flora asked.

"Oh, this is nothing," the small wood duck replied. "This is just an old injury and some dried oil. My family got it much worse. I wasn't with them where they were swimming when the oil came in so fast! They all died in that explosion that your friend, the big bird, talked about."

"How awful," Flora said. "I know how it feels. I lost my parents too."

"I didn't see the big thing explode, but I heard it!" the duck went on. "I was swimming, and I dived under, and when I came up for air, I couldn't see. All I remember after that is darkness. Then, when I woke up, I was in a small glass room with a few other wood ducks. There were people there too. I looked around for my parents, but they weren't there. I heard a human say there was only one duck who had survived from that area. Then I realized they were talking about me, and that my family was gone, and I was overcome with sadness! I cried and cried. I still am sad. But now I'm so much older! I'm two years old now—practically grownup! Well, I don't look so grownup, because I'm small for my age, but I can take care of myself! I just don't know how I'll ever get all this black stuff off my wings. I try and try, but it's glued on!"

"Zolo," The Fluff said. "Let me show you around." Happily, Zolo hopped off the seat to follow his new "Big Brother." Everyone looked at each other.

"I feel sorry for that duck, but he sure can talk," said Edgar.

Acorn Creek

Two days later, the train was rolling through lush green fields of grass and then heavily wooded hills. The girls and animals looked out the open windows into deep ravines with rushing rivers.

As they started to climb, Tomás took a deep breath and sighed, "Mountains."

Just then, they came around a sharp bend, and before them they saw what looked like a giant, hilly sandbox with trucks crawling all over it.

"What's going on here? Where did the mountain go?" Tomás asked.

"That's a coal mine," Marina said. "Coal used to be dug out of deep tunnels inside the mountains, but now, the energy companies just chop the tops off whole mountains to get at the coal."

"Chop the tops off mountains?" Sally squeaked.

"How can they do that?"
Tomás cried. "If they chopped off *my* mountain, they would destroy all the homes my family has ever made, ever since my great, great *abuelitos*—I mean, grandfathers. My mountain has been our home for a long, long time!"

At the bottom of a hollow, the train screeched to a halt, and everyone practically flew out of the windows.

"Yikes, that was abrupt. What a harsh landing!" Joanna remarked as she stood up dizzily. "I guess we'd better see why we stopped."

Tomás and Sally were already outside, peering into a creek. It was a strange reddish-orange color. The others crowded around.

"Ick," Lauren said. "That's the same color as the water back where I used to live."

"Oh, look at the poor little minnows! They're so still. Why don't they swim?" Tomás said. He wanted to scoop them up with his paw, but he didn't want to scare them.

A few feet downstream, the group saw a fish in a sundress, with a hat and a parasol.

Sally ran to talk to her. "What's your name?" she asked.

The fish stopped swimming and looked at the salamander. "Well, good day to y'all! Welcome to Acorn Creek," she said with a drawl. "My name is Bobbi Sue Sunfish. May I offer you refreshments?" she pointed to the river grass. "Forgive me if it's a bit bitter. I'm told that this is what's called 'toxic.' "

"Toxic? Are you okay?" Tomás asked worriedly.

"Does it look like I'm okay?" Bobbie Sue burst out. "Of course I'm not okay! Look at this water! Look at them!" She jabbed her parasol toward the motionless minnows.

"Um . . . I'm so sorry! By the way, I am Tomás," he said.

"And I'm Sally," the salamander said. "We came here on a magic train that brings us from place to place where there are problems with the land."

"And water," Tomás added.

"And air," Sally said. "It seems there are problems everywhere we look!"

"These are our friends," she said, as the others collected around her. "We all joined the train. We're headed to Washington, D.C., to tell the Mister President of the United States about the problems we're having because of—"

"Climate change and pollution!" Inoah chimed in.

"By the way," Edgar asked, "why is this water pink?"

"The water is pink because *someone* poured *something* called fracking fluid into my stream," Bobbi Sue said.

"Oh dear," Creamy said. "How horrible."

"Yes, but what's fracking?" Edgar asked.

"It happens when people use way too much water to push chemicals deep into the ground to get icky oil, and when the water comes back up, it comes back into the stream all gross and red!" Bobbi Sue said. "All to make money!"

"Wait . . . so they get money from the ground?" Sally squeaked.

Inoah sighed loudly. "No, No, No," she squawked. "Incorrect!"—then added under her breath, "Why do I have to explain everything?"

Joanna shifted Inoah off her shoulder and onto the ground, but the bird merely ruffled her feathers and continued: "Hydraulic fracturing is a process whereby energy companies inject water and chemicals into the ground at high pressure to force natural gas—or methane—out of the rock."

"Oh, so they can sell it for money?" Bobbi Sue asked.

"Correct!" Inoah said.

"But what *are* these chemicals?" Edgar chimed in.

"That, my friend, is a secret!" Inoah squawked.

"Whatever it is, it's making me and my friends very ill," Bobbi Sue said. "This river used to be what was

called an 'outstanding water resource.' That means it used to be the cleanest in the state. My mamma and papa were always so proud that we lived here. We were really lucky that the coal mines didn't pollute the water."

The Fluff thought for a moment. "Bobbi Sue," he asked, "would you like to come onboard with us and help us? We all have stories like yours, and we could use you to tell more stories."

"Well, as long as this Washington Mister can help my stream, I'm in!" she declared as she handed him her parasol.

"I have an idea!" Zolo said as he ran in circles and then into the train. Moments later, he came

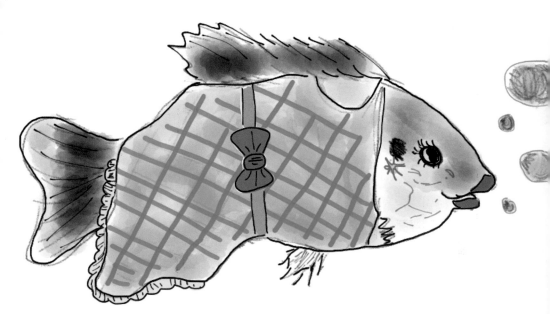

back panting. "I just asked the train to make a fresh-water swimming pool, and it did! So, Bobbi Sue, if you'd like to join us, we have a place for you to stay."

Creamy madly waved her flipper in the air and said, "We should make a food bar next to the pool so Bobbi Sue can get food whenever she wants."

"Ooooo ooooo!" Zolo said. "We all can use the pool too! That is, those of us who like to swim," he added quickly, glancing at Edgar.

"I suppose it's getting late," Edgar said, "and we should get back on the train."

The animals nodded and climbed onboard.

Tomás smiled at the fish. "All right, Bobbi Sue, I'm going to pick you up to carry you now. Okay?"

"All right," she said, "but be careful with those claws."

Moments later, as Bobbi Sue swam around her new pool, she saw The Fluff, Flora, Zolo, Creamy, Joanna, and Marina come to the edge.

"Are you okay with us swimming with you?" Flora asked.

"As long as you mind your manners and don't eat me," Bobbie Sue replied.

The animals nodded solemnly. Zolo was the first one in, splashing as Bobbi Sue dove out of the way.

Back in the car, Edgar and Tomás sat together. Tomás gestured to Edgar as he saw a small yellow bird fly past the window. They began to doze.

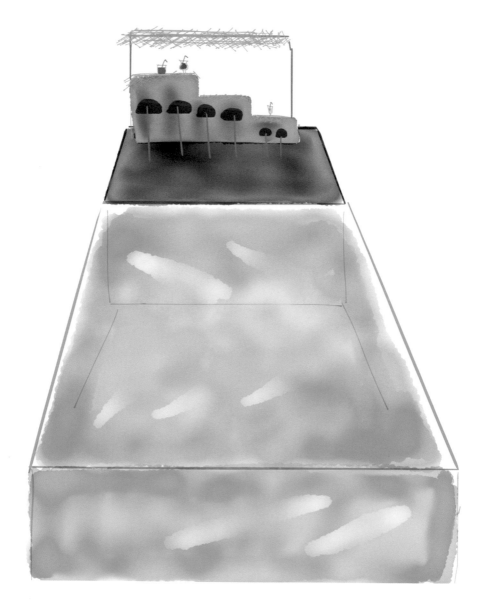

New York City

As the train sped through the countryside, Marina was happy to see some solar arrays, but there were also many fracking wells.

She sat back in her seat and sighed, "We have to get to the president, and fast."

At that thought, the train began moving so quickly the view outside the window became a blur.

In less than an hour, everyone onboard could see a city skyline. The train began to slow down.

"Oh look!" Joanna exclaimed, "I think we're heading into New York City!"

"Well, since we're here, let's go look around!" Marina added excitedly.

"Okay," The Fluff said, "Let's do it!"

The girls and animals had an early picnic dinner in Central Park, and then, at Flora's suggestion, attended the Broadway musical *The Lion King*. Coming out of the play at Times Square, they stopped to watch street performers break dancing and doing gymnastic tricks in the center of the square.

Sally was unimpressed. "I don't see why people are giving them money. I could easily do that with my eyes closed. Watch!"

She did a flip on Marina's hand.

"Wait," Joanna said. "I'll get something so that people can see you."

She headed over to an abandoned box leaning up against a parking meter. As she picked up the dusty cardboard, she saw a dark shape under it.

"Eeeeeeekkkkkkk! A rat!" she shrieked.

Standing up on his hind legs, the rat look cool, calm, and collected. He was wearing a tie-dyed shirt and tie-dyed pants with a large peace sign on the left leg. Dreadlocks came down to his shoulders, and in a pointy ear shone a single gold earring.

"What's all the fuss, girlfriend? You'd think you never saw a rat before. Jeeeessshhhh," said the rat, crossing his arms and frowning impatiently, giving

Joanna the once-over. "You have some nerve! You've taken away my perfectly good hideout, carefully placed in the middle of all this people food. I demand that you replace it immediately, and give me some of that pretzel in your hand for my trouble."

In shock, Joanna quickly gave him half of her giant pretzel, mumbling an apology.

"Thanks," the rat said "By the way, Zingo's the name. And who are you and this traveling zoo?"

"Hey!" Creamy said. "We are not a zoo!"

"Yeah," said Edgar, "and we're a lot bigger than you!"

"Speak for yourself," squeaked Sally. "But you ruined my street performance!"

"Street performance?" Zingo snorted. "What are you guys even doing here?"

"We're here because global warming is threatening all of our homes, and we want to talk to the president about it," Flora said.

"This is Flora," said Tomás. "I'm Tomás, and this is my best friend Sally, and this is Lauren, Creamy, Edgar, Marina, The Fluff, Joanna, and—"

"Hi! I'm Zolo!"

The little duck ran eagerly over to Zingo. "I'm a wood duck. I'm two years old! You look weird. Oh look! I feel like I'm *finally* bigger than someone! Except for Sally, of course. She's a salamander. We came here on a magic train. It took us a long time to get from Texas to here. Isn't that amazing? The Fluff and Creamy started in San Diego. I think it's really cool. How about you? Where do you live? Do you want to join us on the train? I like your shirt. Do you know where I can get one like it? Is there anywhere to go swimming near here?"

Booom! A crash of thunder rolled across the sky. In seconds, the entire group was drenched as rain came down in sheets. People were running for cover, hailing cabs, and getting on buses.

Zingo took charge. "Follow me, you guys! I got a great place to wait out the storm."

The animals and girls followed at a run. Zingo led them to an alley between two restaurants where a fire escape overhead protected them.

Zingo frowned and looked skyward. "Hmmmmm," he said. "This isn't good. Can you guys feel the air? Something's up. I don't think we're seeing the end of this weather anytime soon."

"Yes, it feels like it does just before a huge snowstorm!" Flora said.

The animals all nodded in agreement and began talking at once.

Zolo interrupted: "I don't know what snow is, but I sure know about storms! Once when I—"

The Fluff hurriedly picked him up, still talking, and clapped a flipper over his mouth.

"We have to get back to the train," Marina cried out.

Another rumble sounded through the buildings of Times Square. As lightning lit the sky, a vehicle appeared before them, streaming with rain but surrounded by bubbles and butterflies.

It was the train!

"Whoah . . . cool. What a train," Zingo said approvingly.

"Let's go!" Marina shouted.

"Let's go?" said Zingo. "On this? Niiiiice! This is even better than those flower power buses they had in the '60s."

He followed along with his eyes shining as everyone crowded onboard.

The Storm

By midnight, the storm was raging. The train rocked back and forth like a ship on an angry sea.

"Hold on tight, everybody!" The Fluff called out.

All at the same time, bad things started happening all over the Big Apple. The lights went out in

Lower Manhattan; 140-mph winds knocked out streetlights, downed power poles, and ripped out trees; torrents of rain flooded rooftops and awnings. But the worst was the ocean.

The Global Warming Express sped toward the south end of Manhattan Island. In less than a minute, the train had reached Battery Park, where seawater was pouring in. Instantly, a huge wall of water surged up over the train, bringing it to a halt. But instead of being swamped, the train just . . . floated!

All the animals sat down on the floor in shock. Marina and Joanna stood peering out the windows into the dark sky, trying to see what was happening.

Sally was the first to speak. "What's going on?" she asked.

Zolo jumped up on a seat and started dancing as he said: "Wow! This is awesome and amazing. I really love this! Where are we? Wow! So much water!"

The Fluff brought him down to earth by squashing him back into his seat. "Zolo, we're in the middle of a huge storm. I wouldn't be dancing if I were you," The Fluff said as he put Zolo's seatbelt on him, firmly.

Just as The Fluff looked up, a roaring sound filled the cars. Everyone looked out in horror.

"Oh my gosh!" Joanna called out. "This isn't just a big storm. It's a hurricane! We all have to sit down and buckle up *now*!"

As the hurricane swept the train into the sky, the screen rolled down, swinging wildly across the windows. The train was being tossed up and down, turned around, and thrown back and forth. Objects were flying all over it. Zolo clung on to The Fluff with his eyes shut tight. Suddenly, the freezer door flew open, and a frozen fish flew across the car, hitting The Fluff in the head. He was out cold.

The girls and animals all were terrified. The younger ones, like Sally and Zolo, started running around the car in panic. This made the others even more scared, and most of them started crying.

"*Screeeeeeeeaauukk!*"

"What was that?" Creamy asked, her eyes wide. Immediately everyone got very quiet, and the young animals stopped running.

"It's going to be okay," they heard Marina say. All eyes were on her. The animals saw that Joanna was comforting Inoah. Had that horrible noise been Inoah crying? They'd never heard her cry.

"I know . . . all the . . . facts, but I . . . never really . . . understood . . . how . . . how . . . ," Inoah gasped in between sobs.

"How what?" Joanna asked, hugging Inoah.

"How bad it really is!" Inoah finally said.

Zingo stroked his scraggly beard, deep in thought.

As Joanna comforted Inoah, the other animals noticed movement at the other end of the car. The Fluff was waking up.

When he came to, he felt a sharp pain in his head and saw blurry shapes all around him. As his vision cleared, he saw the other animals peering down at his face, worried.

"Thank goodness," Flora said. "I thought you were dead!"

The Fluff sat up and pointed to the screen. "Look!"

The screen was showing TV news saying, "Super Storm Sandy has just hit New York City at Battery Park with a fourteen-foot wave. This is the storm as seen from outer space."

Then the screen showed video footage of the storm as it looked from a satellite. When it was over, Marina realized that the train wasn't rocking anymore. "Wow," she said. "It's so peaceful here. We must be in the eye of the storm."

"What's the eye of a storm?" The Fluff asked with big eyes as he nibbled his frozen fish.

"It's the inside of the hurricane," Inoah squawked as she wiped the tears off her feathers.

"Weird," Flora said. "Look! Blue sky! The eye is so different from the rest of the storm." She unbuckled her seatbelt to walk over to the window.

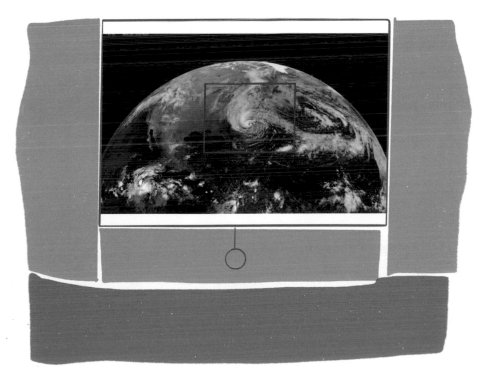

Creamy joined her. "Look at the clouds all around us. They're so so so so big!"

The two sat down again, their eyes filled with wonder. Absentmindedly, they buckled their seat belts again—only just in time.

Bang! They had hit the wall of the storm's eye. The train was suddenly tossed in the air as if it weighed nothing. Then, just as suddenly, it flew down to Earth, landed on what was left of the pavement, and started speeding through New York City again.

The storm was over, but much of the city was ruined. The screen showed them images of destruction

from all over New York. Even the Statue of Liberty and Ellis Island had been affected.

"Oh, my!" Flora cried. "What a terrible mess!"

Creamy started crying again, as everyone saw the city houses, buildings, subways, and parks that had been flooded or ruined. Inoah started to cry—or screech—again. "It's no use," she sobbed. "I don't think this can be fixed just by seeing the president."

Zingo suddenly stood up on a chair and declared: "You're right! You can't just leave this to the president. He may be in charge, but he's only one dude. Real change takes a movement, a happening, a whole new mindset. *You* have to act. Because of climate change, this storm is one of the biggest to ever hit the East Coast," he said, shaking his fist. "It's your responsibility to create your own wonderful future! You guys can do this! I know you can! Look how far you've come already!"

He pumped his fist in the air, and the animals all cried out in agreement.

"Now I need to leave you," he said. "I have to see how my home held up. But remember: You guys have the power to fix this problem. Take it from someone who knows how to change in order to survive. Goodbye!"

"Goodbye!" cried all the animals. "Good luck, Zingo!" They watched as he slipped out through a crack near the door and disappeared.

103

The girls were hugged and hugged, and all six humans were surrounded by all the animals. All, that is, except Bobbi Sue, who was peering at the action with her face up against the glass of her train car.

Once Joanna and Marina had greeted their parents, they introduced the animals.

"Where did you find all these friends?" Marina's dad asked, watching as the animals inched closer to the parents, obviously curious but a little unsure.

"Well, the train found a way to lead us to all these animals because they needed help," Joanna explained. "They've all lost their habitats or families—or both—because of climate change."

Chipper trotted over to Creamy, who, taken by surprise, toppled over. After she got up, Chipper gave her a sympathetic head tilt. Creamy smiled and gave the dog a hug.

The grownups all looked worried, and Marina's mom asked, "Are they okay now?"

"Well, that's why we're here," Marina motioned to the White House. "They still need help for their homes."

"So, do you mean to tell us that you've been traveling with all these animals across the country in a train?" Joanna's mom asked.

"Also Canada!" Inoah interjected.

Joanna's mom looked startled. "*That's* why it's been so quiet at home," she exclaimed. "Inoah was with *you!*"

"One question," Marina said. "How did you know we were here?"

"Well," Marina's mom replied, "Little Croissant has been telling us where you were."

"Who's Croissant?" Joanna asked.

Before her mom could say anything, a yellow canary wearing a tiny blue beret landed on Joanna's head. The animals all looked at each other in surprise, and Joanna held out her hand to let him sit there.

"Oh wait! We saw him!" Marina cried out. "Joanna, remember? Every time we stopped at a new location, we saw a blur of yellow flash past the window!"

"Croissant, was that you? Were you tracking us all this time and helping our parents to know everything?" Joanna laughed, with her face close to the little bird's.

Croissant peeped loudly, nodded his head up and down vigorously enough to shake his tiny beret, and then puffed up his chest with pride. Everyone laughed.

"He must have been following you," Marina's dad said. "We were all given notes about your journey by this little bird, starting on the day you left. They were all signed, 'Croissant, from the Pastry Express.'"

"Oh, so you weren't worried?" Marina said.

"Well, we were still worried," Marina's mom answered. "I mean, it isn't every day that your kids take off on a train powered by bubbles!"

"And butterflies," Joanna laughed, pointing to the hundreds of monarch butterflies flying around the garden, looking for milkweed.

"Anyway, when we heard you were in New York City during the storm, we were really worried, so we decided to fly out immediately," Joanna's dad said.

Croissant

"See, we saved the notes Croissant brought us," Marina's mom said, holding up a thick bunch of small, bright yellow sticky notes.

Suddenly, the parents realized that the polar bear had started to grumble. "What did she say?" Joanna's dad asked.

"She asked, 'What do we do now that we're here?'" Marina answered.

"How can you can understand them?" Joanna's mom said and looked at the animals.

"I'm not sure," Joanna said. At that moment, Sally started to cry.

"Oh, what's the matter?" Marina's dad asked, concern spreading on his face.

"She says," Marina translated, "that she can't believe she was fortunate enough to"—her eyes got watery, and Joanna picked up the translation—"to find a group of friends who cared so much about her and risked their lives to help her." Joanna finished, trying to hold back her tears, and then she ran over to pick up Sally into her hand. The parents smiled kindly as Marina dried her tears.

"I also can't believe how lucky I am to have found you guys!" Lauren piped up.

"Wait," Joanna's mom said. "I understood that!" The parents all agreed and smiled at each other.

"I'm lucky too!" cried The Fluff.

"Me too!" all the animals exclaimed and hugged each other, the girls, and the parents. When everyone had dried their happy tears, the animals started to nudge each other.

Everyone looked to where the animals were pointing excitedly. It was the entrance to the White House.

"They are saying, they are saying . . . . Oh, my word! That's the president!" Marina exclaimed.

And she was right. The president of the United States of America was standing on the White House steps, smiling. He was waving his hand in the air, and in it he held a bright yellow sticky note—Croissant had been visiting him too.

Resources

Dr. James Hansen, director, Climate Science, Awareness and
Solutions Program, Earth Institute, Columbia University:
https://www.ourchildrenstrust.org
https://www.ted.com/talks/james_hansen_why_i_must
https://www.youtube.com/watch?v=JP-cRqCQRc8

Earth Care International:
http://earthcare.nationbuilder.com

Earth Guardians:
http://www.earthguardians.org

Environmental Protection Agency:
https://www.epa.gov

i Matter Youth:
http://www.imatteryouth.org

Jeff Orlowski, film director, *Chasing Ice*:
https://www.youtube.com/watch?v=hC3VTgIPoGU
http://earthvisioninstitute.org

Just Right Climate:
http://justrightclimate.org

National Aeronautics and Space Administration:
https://climate.nasa.gov//

National Oceanic and Atmospheric Administration:
www.noaa.gov

New Energy Economy:
http://www.newenergyeconomy.org

Our Children's Trust:
https://www.ourchildrenstrust.org

Sierra Club:
http://sierraclub.org

Sierra Club Rio Grande Chapter:
http://www.riograndesierraclub.org

Stephanie Jenouvrier, Associate Scientist, Biology, Woods
Hole Oceanographic Institution:
http://www..whoi.edu/profile.do?id=sjenouvrierspeak_out_
about_climate_change

Stuart Pimm, scientist and GWE Advisory Board Member:
http://thepimmgroup.org
https://www.amazon.com/Scientist-Audits-Earth-Stuart-
Pimm/dp/0813535409
http://www.pbs.org/newshour/bb/new-report-suggests-earth-
brink-great-extinction/

*The Melting World: A Journey Across America's Vanishing
Glaciers,* by Christopher White, St. Martin's Press

Young Voices for the Planet: http://www.youngvoices
onclimatechange.com

To contact us at *The Global Warming Express:*
www.theglobalwarmingexpress.org
https://www.facebook.com/theglobalwarmingexpress. org

For information about our award-winning school programs
and camps:
genie@theglobalwarmingexpress.org